The Little Engine That Could™

Retold by Watty Piper
Illustrated by Ruth Sanderson

BARNES
&NOBLE
BOOKS
NEW YORK

Platt & Munk, Publishers • New York
A division of Grosset & Dunlap, Inc.

Designed by Craigwood Phillips, A Good Thing, Inc.

Chug, chug, chug. Puff, puff, puff. Ding-dong, ding-dong.
The little train rumbled over the tracks.
She was a happy little train
for she had such a jolly load to carry.

Her cars were filled full of good things for boys and girls.
There were toy animals—giraffes with long necks,
Teddy bears with almost no necks at all,
and even a baby elephant.

Then there were dolls—dolls with blue eyes and yellow curls,
dolls with brown eyes and brown bobbed heads,
and the funniest little toy clown you ever saw.

And there were cars full of toy engines,
airplanes, tops, penknives, picture puzzles, books,
and every kind of thing boys or girls could want.
But that was not all.

Some of the cars were filled with all sorts of good things
for boys and girls to eat—big golden oranges,
red-cheeked apples, bottles of creamy milk for their breakfasts,
fresh spinach for their dinners,
peppermint drops, and lollypops for after-meal treats.

5

The little train was carrying all these wonderful things
to the good little boys and girls on the other side of the
mountain. She puffed along merrily.

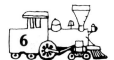

Then all of a sudden she stopped with a jerk.
She simply could not go another inch.
She tried and she tried, but her wheels would not turn.

What were all those good little boys and girls
on the other side of the mountain going to do
without the wonderful toys to play with
and the good food to eat?
"Here comes a shiny new engine,"
said the funny little clown who jumped out of the train.
"Let us ask him to help us."
So all the dolls and toys cried out together:

"Please, Shiny New Engine,
won't you please pull our train over the mountain?
Our engine has broken down, and the boys and girls

on the other side won't have any toys to play with
or good food to eat unless you help us."

11

But the Shiny New Engine snorted: "I pull you?
I am a Passenger Engine. I have just carried a fine big train
over the mountain, with more cars than you ever dreamed of.
My train had sleeping cars, with comfortable berths;

a dining-car where waiters bring whatever
hungry people want to eat;

and parlor cars in which people sit in soft arm-chairs
and look out of big plate-glass windows.
I pull the likes of you?

"Indeed not!"
And off he steamed to the roundhouse,
where engines live when they are not busy.

How sad the little train and all the dolls and toys felt!
Then the little clown called out,
"The Passenger Engine is not the only one in the world.

Here is another engine coming,
a great big strong one. Let us ask him to help us."

The little toy clown waved his flag
and the Big Strong Engine came to a stop.
"Please, oh, please, Big Engine," cried all the dolls and toys
together. "Won't you please pull our train over the mountain?
Our engine has broken down, and the good little boys and girls

on the other side won't have any toys to play with
or good food to eat unless you help us."
But the Big Strong Engine bellowed: "I am a Freight Engine.

I have just pulled a big train loaded with big machines
over the mountain. These machines print books and newspapers
for grown-ups to read. I am a very important engine indeed.
I won't pull the likes of you!"
And the Freight Engine puffed off indignantly to the roundhouse.

The little train and all the dolls and toys were very sad.

"Cheer up," cried the little toy clown.

"The Freight Engine is not the only one in the world.

Here comes another. He looks very old and tired,
but our train is so little, perhaps he can help us."
So the little toy clown waved his flag and the dingy,
rusty old engine stopped.

"Please, Kind Engine," cried all the dolls and toys together.
"Won't you please pull our train over the mountain?
Our engine has broken down, and the boys and girls on the other
side won't have any toys to play with or good food
to eat unless you help us."

But the Rusty Old Engine sighed: "I am so tired.
I must rest my weary wheels. I cannot pull even so little a train
as yours over the mountain. I cannot. I cannot. I cannot."

And off he rumbled to the roundhouse chugging,
"I cannot. I cannot. I cannot."
Then indeed the little train was very, very sad, and the dolls
and toys were ready to cry.
But the little clown called out, "Here is another engine coming,

a little blue engine, a very little one,
maybe she will help us."
The very little engine came chug, chugging merrily along.
When she saw the toy clown's flag, she stopped quickly.

"What is the matter, my friends?" she asked kindly.
"Oh, Little Blue Engine!" cried the dolls and toys.
"Will you pull us over the mountain?

Our engine has broken down
and the good boys and girls on the other side
won't have any toys to play with or good food to eat,
unless you help us. Please, please, help us, Little Blue Engine."

"I'm not very big," said the Little Blue Engine.
"They use me only for switching trains in the yard.
I have never been over the mountain."
"But we must get over the mountain before the children awake,"
said all the dolls and the toys.

The very little engine looked down and saw the tears in the dolls'
eyes. And she thought of the good little boys and girls
on the other side of the mountain
who would not have any toys or good food unless she helped.

Then she said, "I think I can. I think I can. I think I can."
And she hitched herself to the little train.
The toy clown jumped aboard
and all the dolls and the toy animals began to smile and cheer.

She tugged and pulled and pulled and tugged
and slowly, slowly, slowly they started off.

**Puff, puff, chug, chug, went the Little Blue Engine.
"I think I can—I think I can—I think I can—I think I can
—I think I can**

I think I can—I think I can—I think I can—I think I can."
Up, up, up. Faster and faster and faster
the little engine climbed,
until at last they reached the top of the mountain.
Down in the valley lay the city.

34

"Hurray, hurray,"
cried the funny little clown and all the dolls and toys.
"The good little boys and girls in the city will be happy
because you helped us, kind, Little Blue Engine."
And the Little Blue Engine smiled
and seemed to say as she puffed steadily down the mountain,

"I thought I could. I thought I could. I thought I could.
I thought I could.

I thought I could.

I thought I could.”

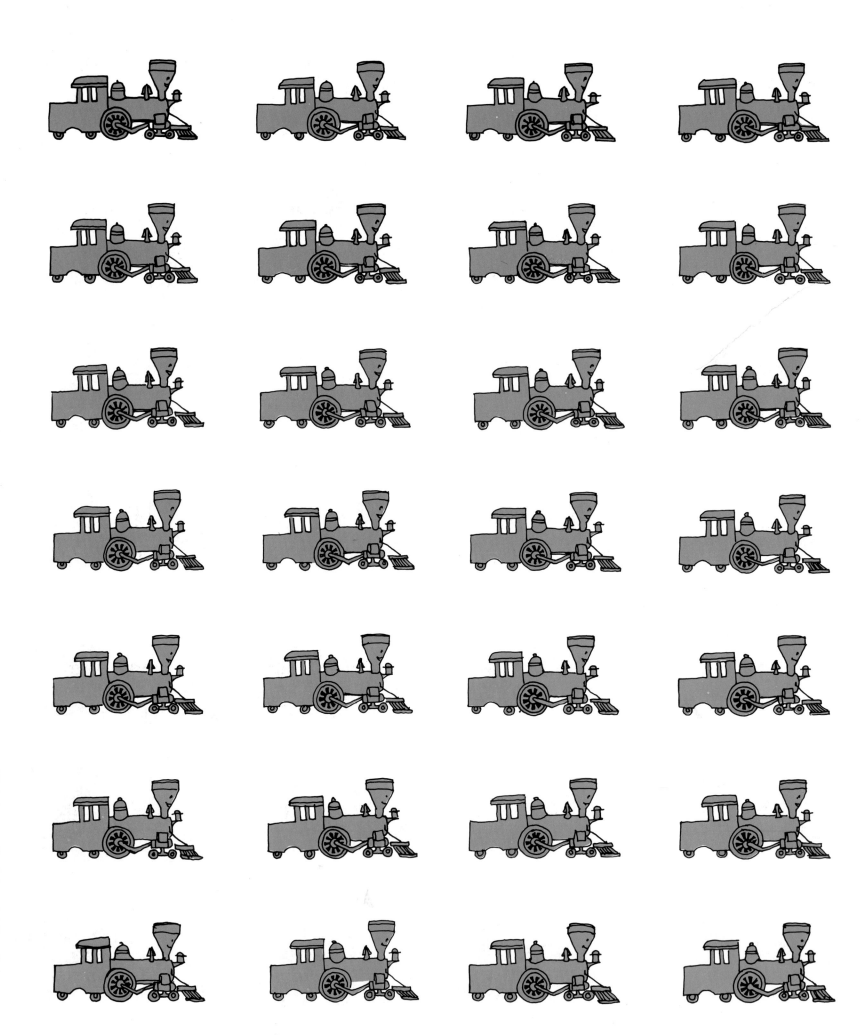